Raccoon Wants to Be First

SUSANNA
ISERN

LEIRE
SALABERRIA

nubeOCHO

Raccoon lives in the forest.

His favorite things to do are swinging from his striped tail, doing somersaults on the grass with his friends and climbing up to the tops of trees to watch the moon.

Ever since he was very little, Raccoon stood out from all the other animals for being very skillful: at harvest time, he always got the first hazelnut.

When looking for a four leaf clover, he was the first to find one and he always got the highest points playing guess the cloud shapes.

Raccoon is almost always the first in everything, and many look at him with admiration. Whenever that happens, he fluffs his tail out proudly.

As time goes by, everyone knows Raccoon wants to be the first in everything!

He trains long and hard in order to be the fastest and the smartest animal in the forest.

He plays games with his eyes closed and his tummy full, and easily wins. He works hard, from sunrise to sunset, to be the best.

One day, a fox from another forest comes to Raccoon's forest and quickly becomes friends with the animals of his age. While they lounge in the shadows of trees, he tells them incredible stories:

"Beyond the river there is an immense ocean. I was the first of my group to discover it."

"On one occasion, I encountered a dangerous shark, famous for its lethal bite. Never before has a land mammal survived to tell this story!"

One afternoon, while Fox was recounting his adventures, a gust of wind carried off Squirrel's favorite hat and dropped it in the deepest part of the river.

Without thinking twice, Raccoon jumped into the water to get it.

But Fox also had the same idea. He jumped in the water like an arrow and caught the hat.

Raccoon wasn't the first that time, and he didn't like it.

Another day, after it had rained, the animals were having fun leaping over puddles.

Raccoon saw an enormous puddle in the distance. He started to run so he could be the first to reach it and make an impressive leap.

However, Fox had also seen it and jumped from branch to branch with such agility that he overtook Raccoon. Raccoon started to run faster but tripped on a rock and fell flat on his face in the muddy water.

The animals burst out laughing. Raccoon, dirty and furious, disappeared behind the trees.

Since then, Raccoon has been alone
and sulking.

His friends try to cheer him up,
but Raccoon won't listen to them.

Fox is too good for him to compete with.
If he can't be the first in everything,
Raccoon doesn't want to play.

Big bear cave

Start

Forest

Mountain top

Centenary turtle land

Pine Bridge

Clover meadow

Grand River

Lynx watching site

Crocodile lake

Like every year, with the arrival of the good weather, the young animals organize a climb to the top of the nearest mountain.

Once, Raccoon would have stayed awake all night so he could set off very early the next morning and be the first to get to the top. But now that Fox is going, Raccoon isn't interested in climbing the mountain.

Raccoon stayed behind, but he was not the only one. Duck is crying beside the river. On seeing him, Raccoon approaches his friend:

"What's the matter, Duck? Why didn't you go with the others?"

"I am always the last and I'm afraid of getting lost like last year."

"Don't cry any more," Raccoon says, after thinking about it for a while. "I'll go with you. I won't leave you alone."

The two animals began to climb the mountain. Raccoon had never gone up the mountain at such a slow pace, but for the first time he didn't mind.

"Isn't that the solitary old albino Lynx?" Raccoon asks, thrilled by his discovery.

"Yes, he usually hides in the branches of those trees. You need to look very carefully, because he is camouflaged among the white flowers," Duck explains.

"I've never seen him before. When I went through here, my feet ran so fast that my eyes couldn't stop to look at anything."

At midday, they sat down to eat beside a lake with a waterfall. Butterflies fluttered everywhere. Birds and frogs sang.

The sun shone brightly and the breeze blew gently.

"I always ate so quickly before. I never noticed what I was missing out on...," Raccoon sighed.

Later, they encountered a turtle, flat on his back and wriggling his legs. The two friends helped him to turn over. The turtle nodded his thanks and continued on his way, unhurriedly. This made Raccoon think.

At sunset, Raccoon and Duck still hadn't reached the summit.

"I can't go on," Duck admitted, exhausted. "You'll have to go on without me."

"One last push," Raccoon encouraged his friend. "There's not far to go."

"I'm sorry. I can't," Duck lamented, with his tongue hanging out from his beak.

When the night starts to fall, and although he can only move very slowly, Raccoon keeps climbing up the mountainside.

All the animals watch him from the summit,
very surprised. When he finally reaches the top,
they all rush toward him, as if he were a hero.

Raccoon smiles, proudly. Not being first has more advantages than he had thought.

One of them is that there is always someone waiting to greet you with a big hug!